Text and illustrations copyright © 1992 by Elaine Greenstein.
Published by Picture Book Studio, Saxonville, MA.
Distributed in the United States by Simon & Schuster.
Distributed in Canada by Vanwell Publishing, St. Catharines.
All rights reserved.
Printed in Hong Kong.
1 2 3 4 5 6 7 8 9 10

Library of Congress Cataloging in Publication Data
Greenstein, Elaine
Emily and the crows / written and illustrated by Elaine Greenstein.
p. cm.
Summary: In order to get near enough to find out why Emily the cow
is always surrounded by cackling crows, Ivy learns to act like a crow
herself and finally learns the secret.
ISBN 0-88708-238-6 : $14.95
[1.Crows—Fiction. 2.Cows—Fiction.] I.Title.
PZ7.G8517Em 1992
[E]—dc20   91-39917
CIP
AC

For Julie

Emily and the Crows

Picture Book Studio

Elaine
Greenstein

Every morning Ivy looked out her window at the farm next door.
There was a farmhouse and a barn full of cows.
After the farmer fed the cows their breakfast,
he opened the pink doors and let them out into the fields.

Ivy's favorite cow was named Emily.

Emily always stood away from the other cows,

but she was never by herself.

She was surrounded by crows all the time.

Sometimes the crows were quiet,

and other times they flapped their wings and cackled and cawed.

Crows always do that, but why were they standing near Emily?

Ivy wondered and wondered.
So she borrowed her father's binoculars and looked from far away.
She could see Emily and the crows, but she didn't learn anything new.

Ivy walked out to the field and stood behind a tree near Emily.
When the crows saw her, they all flew away.

The next day Ivy tried again, but the same thing happened.
Whenever she got too close, all the crows flew away.

But they always came flying back to be near Emily,
and Ivy still didn't know why.

As Ivy watched the crows, she had an idea.
She watched them flap their wings and hop around near Emily.
She saw how they tilted their heads,
and she listened carefully as they cackled and cawed.

Then Ivy went home and practiced acting like a crow.

She flapped her arms and she walked like a crow.

She cackled and cawed, and tilted her head.

She practiced until she was just like a crow.

Ivy went back to the field.

She crouched down and slowly went closer to Emily and the crows.

The crows all flew away when they saw her.

So Ivy practiced harder.

She made crow noises and she flapped her wings.

Her mom asked her what she was doing.

"I'm being a crow. Can't you see my feathers?" Her mom smiled.

Ivy practiced cackling and flapping and hopping and cawing every day for a week. Finally Ivy knew she was ready.

Out in Emily's field,
Ivy got closer to the crows than she ever had before.
She was very happy and proud of herself.

To Ivy's surprise, Emily was talking.
Emily was telling a story about pigs—
pigs with wings that flew and ate peaches.
Now Ivy knew why the crows were always around Emily.
Emily told them stories.

Ivy moved close to the other crows.
They nodded to her and she nodded back.
Ivy tilted her head and listened to the story with the others.

At the end of the story all the crows cackled and flapped their wings.
Ivy was so delighted she forgot about flapping her wings
and clapped her hands instead.

The noise startled everyone. All the crows looked at Ivy.
They shrieked and looked scared, and some flew away.

Emily said, "Please! Calm down, everyone!
There's nothing to be afraid of."
Emily asked Ivy her name, then introduced her to the crows.
Emily complimented Ivy on her crow imitation
and invited her to join them.

Ivy sat down and listened while Emily told a story
about the summer the vegetables grew and grew.
The vegetables grew so large that the tomatoes were bigger than Ivy.

Emily's story seemed so real
that Ivy and the crows had to make room for the vegetables.

When the story was finished, Ivy clapped and the crows flapped.
Ivy laughed and the crows cackled.

Just then Ivy's mother called her to come home.
Ivy said good-bye to Emily and the crows,
and Emily invited Ivy to join them again.

That night when Ivy's mother came to tuck her into bed,
she asked which bedtime story Ivy wanted to hear.
Ivy said, "Tonight I'll tell you a story."

Ivy told her mother Emily's story about the flying pigs.
Her mother loved the story,
and when it was finished she laughed and clapped.
She said, "That's a wonderful story, Ivy. Did you make it up yourself?"

Ivy said, "Emily told me,"
as her head sank into the pillow and she fell asleep.